5356 2351

W9-AVI-756

WITHDRAWN

New York Times Best-Selling Authors
Henry Winkler & Lin Oliver

HANK

A Short Tale about a Long Dog

ILLUSTRATED BY SCOTT GARRETT

Grosset & Dunlap
An Imprint of Penguin Group (USA) LLC

Indya, Ace, and Lulu—you all inspire me.
And to Stacey, always—HW

For Bronson Day Bahador, for the happiness
you have brought to us all—LO

For Jakki, a true HW fan!—SG

GROSSET & DUNLAP
Published by the Penguin Group
Penguin Group (USA) LLC, 375 Hudson Street, New York, New York 10014, USA

USA I Canada I UK I Ireland I Australia I New Zealand I India I South Africa I China

penguin.com
A Penguin Random House Company

Text copyright © 2014 by Henry Winkler and Lin Oliver Productions, Inc.
Illustrations copyright © 2014 by Scott Garrett. All rights reserved.
Published by Grosset & Dunlap, a division of Penguin Young Readers
Group, 345 Hudson Street, New York, New York, 10014.
GROSSET & DUNLAP is a trademark of Penguin
Group (USA) LLC. Printed in the USA.

Typeset in Dyslexie Font B.V.
Dyslexie Font B.V. was designed by Christian Boer.

Library of Congress Cataloging-in-Publication Data is available.

ISBN 978-0-448-47998-9 (pbk)   10 9 8 7 6 5 4 3 2 1
ISBN 978-0-448-48240-8 (hc)   10 9 8 7 6 5 4 3 2 1

The books in the Here's Hank series are designed using the font Dyslexie. A Dutch graphic designer and dyslexic, Christian Boer, developed the font specifically for dyslexic readers. It's designed to make letters more distinct from one another and to keep them tied down, so to speak, so that the reader is less likely to flip them in their minds. The letters in the font are also spaced wide apart to make reading them easier.

Dyslexie has characteristics that make it easier for people with dyslexia to distinguish (and not jumble, invert, or flip) individual letters, such as: heavier bottoms (b, d), larger than normal openings (c, e), and longer ascenders and descenders (f, h, p).

This fun-looking font will help all kids—not just those who are dyslexic—read faster, more easily, and with fewer errors. If you want to know more about the Dyslexie font please visit the site www.dyslexiefont.com.

CHAPTER 1

"Hank, I can see tiny bits of tuna fish swimming around on your tongue," my sister, Emily, said.

"Then don't look," I told her. "Just listen. My mouth is full of words that are trying to come out."

"Well, the tuna fish is coming out with them. And it's gross."

I put down my fork. Actually, I was looking for an excuse to put it down, anyway. My mom had whipped up another one of her healthy dinners, which looked and tasted like a science experiment. If you ask me, tuna fish and blueberries do not belong together on the same plate.

"Besides, I don't care what you have to say," Emily went on. "Katherine was here first, and that's that."

As she spoke, I noticed that her tongue didn't look so great either. It was all blue from the blueberries. It looked like the entire Smurf family was living in her mouth.

"Emily, honey," my mom cut

in, "Hank has a right to express his opinion."

"That's right," I said. "And my opinion is that this family needs a pet."

"We have a pet, and her name is Katherine," Emily snapped.

"Katherine is an iguana," I answered. "All she does is hiss and catch flies. She can't even play ball. We need a dog."

My dad stopped midbite and gave me a look.

"Who's going to take care of this dog?" he asked. "A pet needs to be fed and walked and washed and taught proper rules of behavior."

"And that's what I want to do," I said. "I can't wait for that job."

"Hank," Emily said with a sigh. "We can't have a dog because Katherine is just a baby. A big dog would scare her. As her mother, that would break my heart."

"Oh, now you're her mother?" I said. "That makes sense, actually, because you look alike. You both have scales on your feet, claws on your hands, and long, sticky tongues that collect insects."

"Hank, that's enough," my mom said. She got up and started to gather the dishes.

Emily got up, too, and headed
to her bedroom. She returned
with Katherine wrapped around
her shoulders like a scarf.

"You're not bringing that
lizard to the table, are you?"
I complained.

"She's a member of this family, too," Emily told me.

The minute Emily sat down in her chair, Katherine whipped out her long tongue and snatched the last bite of my buttered roll. It was the one thing I wanted to eat. I had been saving that bite to drown out the taste of the rest of dinner.

"Hey, Kathy!" I hollered. "Drop that roll right now. It's mine."

It was too late. The roll had disappeared into her scaly iguana body. Katherine smiled at me as if to say, *Tough patooties, kid.*

"You see what I mean, Dad?" I said. "It's not fair that Emily can have that lizard as a pet. She and her roll-stealer hang out in her room after dinner. But what about me? I'm all alone in my room, with nothing to do."

"Actually, Hank," my dad said, "I was thinking we could do some spelling flash cards after dinner."

"No, Dad. Please, not the flash cards again! They don't help me. I know the word one minute, then I forget it the next."

"Hank, you have a spelling test coming up. Don't you want to do well?" he asked.

There it was again. My dad can hardly get through a meal without bringing up school. My grades aren't good. I know that. But school is hard for me. I try to do well, I really do. Everyone, especially my dad, thinks I don't try hard enough. They say I'm funny and a good talker so there's no reason

I shouldn't have better grades.
I can't explain it, either, but
no matter how hard I try, my
report card never improves.

"Let's make a deal, Dad,"
I suggested. "I'll do the flash
cards. I'll try my hardest. And
if I get a good grade on my
test, you take me to the animal
shelter."

"Great idea," Emily said.
"And be sure to leave him
there."

"I think we should listen
to Hank," my mom said.
"A child needs a goal, and
getting a dog is a good one."

"I just want to know who's

going to clean up the poop,"
my dad said.

"I'm your guy, Dad," I said.
"I'm going to get rubber gloves,
a nose clip, and a face mask."

My dad was already up and
heading for the desk drawer
where he keeps the flash cards.
It's my least-favorite drawer
in the house.

"So here's the agreement,
Hank," he said as he pulled
out the box of Dr. Smarty Pants
Fun With Spelling cards. "If
I see improvement in *all* your
grades, we will make that trip
to the animal shelter."

"Wait a minute, Dad. I

thought we were just talking about my spelling test."

"No, Hank. That's not enough. I need to see improvement in all your grades."

"Even math?" I asked.

"Absolutely math."

"Reading, too?"

Now my dad was getting irritated.

"Every subject," he said.

After dinner, my dad and I sat on the couch and opened the box of flash cards. Wouldn't you know it, the very first word on the very first card was impossible to spell. It was *friend.* How was I supposed

to know that the *i* came before
the *e*? I didn't even know there
was an *i* in the word in the
first place.

I messed up the next three
words, too. Okay, the next
ten words. How was I going
to get a dog, if I couldn't
even remember how to spell
such easy words? I didn't have
an answer to that, so I did
what I always do when I have
a problem to solve: I made a
list.

CHAPTER 2

TEN WAYS I CAN IMPROVE MY GRADES
BY HANK ZIPZER

1. Get a new brain.
2. Borrow Emily's brain. It's good at everything.
3. Move to the planet Neptune, where I'm pretty sure they don't have report cards.
4. Write the answers to the math test on the inside of my eyelids.
5. Hang out with a herd of elephants, because elephants never forget. Maybe their good memories will rub off on me.

6. Eat more broccoli. I don't know if it will help my grades, but maybe I'll grow an inch.

7. Do my homework as soon as I get home from school.

8. I take number seven back. I don't want to get too crazy about this.

9. I can't think of anything for number nine.

10. I can't think of a number ten, either. If you have any suggestions, let me know.

CHAPTER 3

Exactly one week after my dad and I spent the whole horrible evening reviewing flash cards, my teacher, Ms. Flowers, handed back our spelling tests.

"Nice work, Hank," Ms. Flowers said as I stuffed the test into my notebook. "I see real improvement."

Improvement? I quickly pulled out the test. Of the fifteen spelling words, I had gotten six right instead of my usual two.

This was a new Hank Zipzer world record.

"Wowee zowee!" I yelled. "I'm almost a genius."

Frankie Townsend, my best friend, reached across the aisle and gave me a high five.

"Way to go, Hankarooney," he said. "Your dad's going to be happy with this."

"That dog is practically yours," Ashley Wong whispered from her seat. Ashley had just moved into my building and had quickly become best friends with Frankie and me.

"The three of you guys are pathetic," Nick McKelty said. He sits in back of me. When

he breathes, I can feel his hot,
stinky sausage breath all over
my neck. "Six out of fifteen
is nothing to celebrate."

"Perhaps you should keep your
eyes on your own paper, Nick,"
Ms. Flowers said, putting his
test down on his desk. "You
missed half the words yourself."
Ms. Flowers returned to the
front of the class and wrote the

following words on the board:
SCIENCE BOOK REPORT DUE
TOMORROW. Katie Sperling
groaned.

"Oh no," she said. "I'm only
halfway done with my book
on volcanoes."

"Then I suggest you spend
some of recess reading,"
Ms. Flowers told her.

I had a bigger problem than
Katie Sperling. I hadn't started
my book. I hadn't even checked
one out of the library. In fact,
I had totally forgotten about
the assignment.

When the recess bell rang,
I went up to Ms. Flowers's desk.

"Ms. Flowers, I have a small

problem," I said, giving her my best smile. I feel that when you've got bad news, you need to show a lot of teeth.

"What is it, Hank?"

"I forgot to check a science book out of the library."

SCIENCE BOOK REPORT DUE TOMORROW

"But, Hank, I reminded you three times that the book report was due tomorrow."

"Yup, I forgot that, too."

"Oh, Hank." She sighed. "What are we going to do with you? We've had this talk before."

"Don't worry, Ms. Flowers. This time I think I have a solution."

"Well, you're very creative," Ms. Flowers said. "I'll be interested to see what it is."

I actually didn't have a solution. As I walked out of the classroom, I tried to come up with one. But nothing came to me. My mind just wandered around like it was lost in a forest.

I was about to give up, when

I passed the fifth-grade bulletin board. At the top in red letters, it said, SHARKS NEVER SLEEP.

Suddenly, an idea came to me. It was a big idea. And it certainly wouldn't be easy to pull off. I was going to need help, that was for sure. But all I could think about was how much I wanted that dog.

I had to try everything to get it.

CHAPTER 4

I asked Frankie and Ashley
to meet me in our clubhouse
at four o'clock. It's not a real
clubhouse. It's a storeroom in
the basement of our apartment
building where we hang out.
They arrived exactly on time.

"Okay, Hankster," Frankie
said. "Let's see this big idea
you have."

I reached into one of the
cardboard boxes labeled
SUMMER VACATION STUFF.

I pulled out a pair of neon yellow flippers, a snorkel, and some goggles. I put on the flippers and slipped the goggles over my face.

"You look an outer-space creature," Ashley said.

Then I reached into a box labeled EMILY'S BABY TOYS and pulled out two stuffed animals. One was a fuzzy purple octopus who she used to call Morton. The other was a creepy-looking jellyfish with rainbow-colored tentacles.

I held Morton in one hand and the jellyfish in the other. Then I stuffed the snorkel into my mouth. Proudly, I strutted

back and forth in front of
Frankie and Ashley.

"What do you think, guys?"
I tried to say.

"Huh? I can't understand
you," Frankie answered.

Of course he couldn't. I took
the snorkel out of my mouth.

"I'm a shark," I explained, "swimming in the ocean with my underwater friends. I'm going to do my report as Shark Boy. I know a whole lot of scientific shark facts. Like, did you know that sharks don't have a single bone in their bodies? And that they can swim forty to sixty miles an hour? And that they have three fins?"

"All of which you are missing," Frankie pointed out.

"And that's where you come in," I said. "I need you to help me make some fins."

"Oh, I love art projects!" Ashley said, jumping off the couch and heading right for our cardboard boxes. She ripped off one of the flaps and tore it into the shape of a triangle.

"Here's a fin," she said.

"I can attach some string to tie it to your body," Frankie said.

"And for a really special touch," Ashley added, "I'll decorate it with blue and green sparkly rhinestones."

"Easy there, Ashweena," I said. "Sharks don't sparkle."

"They do if they want a good grade," she said.

By dinnertime, I had the best shark costume of any second-grader in America. Maybe even the world.

When we got to school the next morning, Ms. Flowers collected everyone's science book report.

"Where is your report, Hank?" she asked as she stood next to my desk.

"Ms. Flowers, you're going to have to see it to believe it," Frankie told her.

"Hank's report is alive," Ashley added. "And it's amazing."

"Amazingly

bad, you mean," Nick McKelty
said with a snort.

"It sounds interesting to
me," Luke Whitman said, taking
his finger out of his nose. That
finger spends most of the day
in there.

Ms. Flowers thought it over.

"Okay," she said. "Why
don't we see what you've come
up with, Hank."

I took my costume and
went into the hall. Ashley
came to help tie on my fins.
While I was slipping into my
flippers and mask, Frankie
went to the front of the class
to introduce me.

"The subject of this book

report is sharks," he said. "And now, coming to you direct from the undersea world is Hank Zipzer, otherwise known as Shark Boy."

I flopped to the center of the classroom. Then I turned in a circle so everyone could get a good look at the sparkly fin that Ashley had made. I began to recite my shark facts. When I saw the blank looks on everyone's faces, I realized that I still had the snorkel in my mouth. No one could understand me. It just sounded like I was blowing bubbles underwater.

I took out the mouthpiece and started again. I said everything I had learned about sharks. When I was finished, the whole class applauded. Well, everyone but you-know-who.

Ms. Flowers said nothing for

what seemed to be a long time. At last, she spoke.

"Well, Hank, that wasn't exactly the way the assignment was supposed to be done."

I felt my heart drop. If she gave me a bad grade, I was never going to get a dog.

"But you really knew your facts," she continued. "And you showed great creativity. For that, I am going to reward you."

"With an A?" I said.

"Yes, Hank. With an A."

My ears couldn't believe what they were hearing. It was my first A ever in my whole life. I smiled at Frankie and Ashley and did a huge fist pump in the

air. Ashley laughed. Frankie
put his hands up like paws and
barked, "Bowwow."

As for me, I did a happy
dance, flippers and all. That
new dog was almost mine.

CHAPTER 5

The next Thursday, report cards came out. My grandpa, Papa Pete, was picking me up at school that day. I came running out the front door, waving the sealed brown envelope in my hands.

"What you got there?" Papa Pete asked, giving me one of his great big bear hugs.

"My report card," I answered. "Let's hurry home so I can show it to Dad."

"Sounds like you're expecting

some good grades," Papa Pete said. "Getting a dog really has motivated you. I'm proud of you, Hankie."

Usually Papa Pete and I stop at my mom's deli, the Crunchy Pickle, for an after-school snack. But that day, I wanted to get right home.

The minute I set foot in our apartment, I handed the envelope to my dad.

"How did I do?" I asked him before he had even finished opening it. "Are the words 'much improved' going to come flying out of your mouth?"

He put his glasses on and looked over my report card for

what seemed to be forever.

"In a few subjects, there was slight improvement," he said at last. "In science, there was a lot of improvement."

I started jumping up and down.

"Cool! When can we go look at puppies?" I was so happy I was practically shouting.

"However . . . ," he went on.

I hate that word, *however*. Nothing good ever comes after it.

"However, Hank, in some important subjects, such as reading and math, your grades have actually slipped."

Papa Pete put his hand on my dad's shoulder.

"You know, Stan," he said, smiling that great smile of his. "I spent my life running the Crunchy Pickle. My sandwiches made a lot of people happy. And the truth is, I had a hard time with math, too. You learn to figure out what you're good at. Then you go full-steam in that direction."

"So what are you suggesting, Pete?" my dad said. "That I just let Hank be lazy and get any grade he wants?"

"He's not lazy," Papa Pete said. "Let him prove it to you by showing he can take care of a dog."

"Yeah!" I exclaimed. "Dad,

I promise you. I will be the best dog-taker-care-of person in the whole entire solar system."

My dad just sat there, scratching his head.

"I have to discuss this with your mother," he said.

"Great, I can hear her in the kitchen," I said. "Let's go ask her."

"You stay here, Hank. This is an adult decision."

"Then you can't leave out Papa Pete," I said, knowing he would take my side. "He's an adult."

"Have been for quite some time now," Papa Pete said.

Papa Pete winked at me as he followed my dad into the kitchen. As for me, all I could do was put my ear against the kitchen door and try to hear what they were saying.

I couldn't hear a word.

CHAPTER 6

WOOF

I only have one thing
to say about what
happened in the kitchen.

ANIMAL SHELTER, HERE I COME!

CHAPTER 7

DOG

When we walked into the animal shelter on 85th Street and Amsterdam, I heard barking. It was like a doggy glee club that was out of tune.

Officer Perez was in charge of the shelter. She had lots of curly hair and looked a little like the French poodle in cage three.

"How will I know which dog to pick?" I asked Officer Perez.

"Oh, you'll know," she said with a smile. "The right dog will give you a sign. It just happens, like magic."

We split up. Each of us took a row. Except Emily. She refused to participate. Instead, she just sat by Officer Perez's desk reading her book, *How to Think Like a Reptile*.

I started down the middle aisle. There were cages stacked two-high on both sides. Each cage held a lost or abandoned dog. I wondered which dog was going to give me a sign. It was definitely not the little guy in the first cage—he was completely hairless except

for tiny tufts coming out of
his ears.

"Sorry, pal," I said
as I passed by him.
"Our family only
has one bald guy,
and that's my
uncle Gary."

I continued down
the aisle, looking in every cage.
I passed a furry little black dog
with white paws and
a white spot on
his chest.
His bottom
teeth stuck out
much farther
than his top
teeth.

"You are going to need braces," I said to him.

He didn't laugh. I moved on.

The dog in the next cage was a boxer. He drooled a lot. It looked like the Hudson River was coming out of his mouth. If we adopted him, he would definitely need a bib.

I passed a cage with the funniest-looking little dog you've ever seen. He looked like a beige hot dog. He had a long tail but definitely came up short in the fur department. And speaking of short, his legs were so short, there was no room for muscles. I couldn't believe those stubby legs were able to hold up that long body of his.

By this time, I had looked at probably twenty dogs. There wasn't one that connected with me.

I turned around and headed back the way I came.

As I passed the cage with the beige hot dog again, he ran to the front of the cage and sat down.

I knelt down slowly. I didn't want to scare him. Then, he put his paw through the bars of the cage and held it out to me. Without even thinking, I took his paw. Before you could say, "Nice to meet you," we were shaking hands.

"What'd I tell you?" a voice said behind me.

I turned around to see Officer Perez smiling at me. "You don't pick them, they pick you."

I looked at the little dog, never letting go of his paw. He was not at all what I had in mind. But I'll tell you this: When a dog gives you a sign, you have to listen.

"Mom! Dad! Emily!" I hollered. "Here he is! I've found him."

All three of them came running. Emily looked in the cage and started to laugh.

"He looks like a corn dog without a stick!" she hooted.

"Let me take him out so you can meet him," Officer Perez said.

"Before we get carried away here," my dad said, "let me remind everyone that small dogs are extremely yappy."

"This little dachshund is still a puppy," Officer Perez said. "Puppies can be trained."

She already had unlocked his cage and was lifting him out. She gently placed him on the floor in front of us. He was so happy to be free. I know this sounds crazy, but it really looked like he was smiling at me.

"You make me smile, too,"

I said, kneeling down right next to him.

With that, he started running in a circle, the way dogs do when they chase their tails. He went faster and faster, until you couldn't see where his head stopped and his tail began.

"Look at him!" I said, holding my sides and laughing. "He looks like a Cheerio."

No sooner had I said those words, than the dog stopped spinning. He looked up at me and wagged his long tail.

"You like that name?" I said to him. "Cheerio?"

He snuggled right into my arms, licking my face like I was an ice-cream cone.

Even my dad had to laugh. And at that moment, I knew that Cheerio would be coming home with us.

CHAPTER 8

On the way home from the animal shelter, we stopped at Pets for U and Me to buy Cheerio's supplies. I picked out a food bowl with a doggy bone on the bottom of it. I got a water bowl, too, and a neon blue collar. My dad got a crate and a sheepskin mat to put inside it. Cheerio picked out a squeaky toy shaped like a banana. My mom arrived at the cash register carrying a big

package of something called
wee-wee pads.

"What are
those?" I asked.
"I've been
reading up on
how to train
a puppy. Cheerio
will have to be
trained to go to the bathroom
outside," she said. "If he starts
sniffing or turning around in
circles, then he probably has
to go. And if we're inside when
this happens, we direct him to
the wee-wee pad. That way,
he'll learn to just go on the pad
when he's inside the house."

"Ewww," Emily groaned.

"You're not putting those gross things down in my room. Katherine would hate them."

"Don't worry," I told her. "Cheerio doesn't want to hang out with you guys, anyway. He's not interested in watching Katherine catch flies."

"Good," Emily said. "Because we're not interested in watching him wee-wee."

When we got home, Cheerio ran around and sniffed the entire apartment. He sniffed every piece of furniture until he found my dad's slippers, which he keeps tucked under his favorite leather chair.

"Oh no, you don't," my dad

said, diving for his slippers. But
Cheerio was fast, and got one
of them in his mouth before my
dad could reach it.

"That's my slipper," my dad
said. "Drop it."

Cheerio didn't. In fact,
he bit down even harder. My
dad reached down to take the

slipper out of Cheerio's mouth.
He pulled, but Cheerio pulled
harder. It was a major tug-of-
war. At last, Cheerio let go. My
dad flew backward and bumped
into the table where my mom
kept her grandmother's glass
vase.

Crash! Boom! Bam!

The vase fell off the table and smashed into a million pieces.

"Now look what you've done," my dad said to Cheerio.

"Actually, Dad, you did it," I pointed out.

"I can see this dog is going to cause a lot of trouble," he answered, shaking his head.

My mom came in from the kitchen carrying a broom and a dustpan.

"Cheerio and I are so sorry about the vase, Mom," I said. "I know it was your grandma's."

"Oh no, Hank. Grandma's vase is in the kitchen cabinet.

I bought that old vase at
a yard sale for fifty cents."

While she swept up the
mess, my dad turned to Cheerio,
who had no idea he had done
anything wrong.

"Don't wag your tail at
me," my dad said to him.
"If you're to be in this family,
you have to follow the Zipzer
rules. No slipper chewing.
No furniture sniffing. Is that
clear?"

Cheerio turned his head to
one side, as if to say, *I have no
idea what you're talking about,
but do you happen to have a
hamburger in your pocket?*

"And while we're at it,

Hank," my dad went on. "There are dog-care rules for you, too. I expect you to walk Cheerio every day. He must always be on a leash. And you are to keep his water bowl full and feed him every day. These are the responsibilities you assume when you get a dog."

"No problem, Dad," I said. "I will be the picture of responsibility, I promise."

I lifted Cheerio into my arms. "Let's go to our room."

"Don't forget to take one of the wee-wee pads," my mom said. "We don't want Cheerio having an accident on the carpet."

"Cheerio says he would never do a thing like that, Mom."

"I didn't hear that dog say one word," Emily snorted.

"That's because you don't speak puppy," I told her. "You only speak lizard."

I went into the kitchen and took a wee-wee pad from the package. Tucking it under one arm, I picked up Cheerio with the other and headed to my room.

Once we were inside, I put him down on the carpet. "Okay, boy, let's play catch," I said.

I tossed the pad on my bed, then went to my desk drawer

to look for my pink rubber ball.
I found it and rolled it across
the rug. Cheerio watched it go
by. Nothing moved but his head.

"Go get it, Cheerio."
He didn't move. He just
stared at me as if to say, *Why
would I want to do that?*

"So you're not a ballplayer,"
I said to him. "That's okay.
What do you want to do
instead?"

He trotted over to the corner of my room and sniffed around.

"What are you looking for?" I asked him.

He answered me by lifting his leg. I think we all know what happened next.

"Wait, Cheerio. You can't pee there!" I shouted. "You have to go on the wee-wee pad, which is . . . oh no . . . on my bed. I forgot to put it down!"

Cheerio continued to go about his business. The puddle spread halfway across my room. As I watched it sink into the carpet, I had only one thought and it was this: *Uh-oh, Hank Zipzer, you are in big trouble now.*

CHAPTER 9

When he was finished peeing, Cheerio wagged his tail and looked at me happily. He had no idea he had done anything wrong.

"You wait here," I said to him. "I'll go get help."

I opened the door and tiptoed into the living room. "Mom," I whispered. "I have a little problem. Can I talk to you in the kitchen? I don't want to disturb Dad."

"Don't worry about that, Hank," my dad said from his chair. "What's on your mind?"

I had no choice. I took a breath and began.

"Cheerio peed in my room," I said. "All over the carpet."

"What happened?" my mom asked.

"Did you forget to put the wee-wee pad down?" my dad asked me.

"I meant to put it down, Dad. My brain just didn't remember."

"Okay, Hank," he said with a sigh. "I think it's best if Cheerio doesn't spend any more time in your room—at least until you can be more responsible."

"But, Dad, it's almost time for bed. Where's he going to sleep?"

"We'll put his crate in the kitchen, and he'll sleep there," he answered.

"All alone? He'll be so sad."

"He'll be fine," my dad said. "That's what you do when you're training a puppy. And as for you, I believe you have some cleanup work to do in your room."

My mom helped me clean the carpet with tons of paper towels and a special spray that would stop Cheerio from peeing there again. While we were doing that, my dad got Cheerio and put him in his crate in the kitchen.

"Can I at least say good night to him?" I asked when I had finished cleaning up.

"Of course," my dad said.
"Just make it short. It's been
an exciting day. Both you and
Cheerio need to get some rest."

I went into the kitchen and
knelt down by Cheerio's crate.
His tail wagged when
he saw me.

"Good night, boy," I said.
"We'll go on a nice walk
tomorrow. I promise. It will be
morning before you know it."

With one last look at him,
I turned out the lights and went
to my room.

As I climbed into bed, I could
hear Cheerio crying for me.

"Cheerio, that's enough!"
my dad yelled. "Go to sleep."

I lay there in bed, thinking of poor little Cheerio alone in the kitchen. He was there because of me. If only I had remembered to put down that pad, maybe I could have kept his crate in my room, right next to my bed.

I couldn't sleep. Listening to Cheerio cry was just too sad. Then I remembered that the store owner at Pets for U and Me had said to put a piece of my clothing into Cheerio's crate.

If it smelled like me, Cheerio would feel like I was there with him.

So I crept out of bed and pulled a Mets sock from the

dirty-laundry hamper. I sniffed it. Oh yeah, that was me, all right.

I tiptoed into the kitchen. Cheerio was lying in his crate, his little nose sticking through the front gate. The minute he saw me, he almost did a backflip. I slid my fingers as far as I could into his crate, and felt his wet tongue licking them. Boy, that felt good. Cheerio whimpered a little louder.

"I miss you, too, puppy,"

I said. "Here, I've brought something so you won't be so lonely."

I held up my sock for him to smell. He stuck his nose into them and took a big whiff. Then his tail started to wag like crazy. He was the only living thing on the planet who liked the way my sock smelled.

"Okay, boy," I whispered. "I'll just open the door and put it right next to you. Keep very quiet so you don't wake Dad."

As soon as I opened the door just a crack, he shot out of there like a jet plane.

"Cheerio! Get back here!" I yell-whispered.

He didn't listen. He pushed open the kitchen door and disappeared.

I followed him as fast as I could. I couldn't see him in the dark, but I could hear the clicking of his toenails on the wood floor. He was running in giant circles all around the dining-room table.

"Cheerio, please don't do this now," I said to him. "You're going to get us both in trouble."

He never stopped circling the table for one second. I tried to catch him, but he whizzed right by me, his ears flapping behind him.

I ran back into the kitchen and grabbed the bag of dog treats we had bought for him.

When I came back to the dining room, I shook the bag as quietly as I could.

"I have a cookie for you, Cheerio," I whispered.

Suddenly, he came screeching to a stop right in front of me.

I ripped open the bag and took out a treat. Holding it in front of his nose, I backed into the kitchen. He followed, never taking his eyes off that cookie. I put it inside his crate next to my sock. He dove in and gobbled down that treat in one bite. I locked the door as quickly as I could.

It was really late by then. I had to get to bed, but I hated to leave him all alone. I flicked on the TV that sits on the kitchen counter.

"This will keep you company," I said, flipping through the channels. I didn't want him watching the news—it was too scary. And the jewelry channel was definitely too boring. I found some all-night cartoons that he seemed to like.

"I love you," I whispered into his cage.

The last thing I heard as
I crept back to my bedroom
was a happy little doggy yawn.
I smiled. It felt really good
to know I had made Cheerio
feel at home.

CHAPTER 10

The next day at school, all I thought about was Cheerio. I'm usually pretty bad about paying attention. Like when Principal Love is talking on the loudspeaker, I always stare at the clouds outside, wondering if ants could build a colony in them.

After school, my dad came to pick me up. When I saw him, I was totally surprised. He was holding a leash, and at the end of it was my new dog.

"Cheerio!" I called out.

"Hey, is that your dog?"
Nick McKelty said as he tripped
down the front steps. "He's
really short."

"But very cute," Katie Sperling
said. Katie has loved animals ever
since we were in preschool.

Everyone wanted a chance to
pet him, but all Cheerio wanted
was to see me. He tugged on
the leash
and stood
up on his
hind legs,
panting. I
ran to him
and knelt
down,

letting him kiss me all over my face.

"Taking Cheerio on a walk together was a great idea, Dad," I said. "Why don't we take him to the park? The fresh air will be good for all of us."

"You might be right, Hank," my dad answered. "I just read an article that says exercise can sharpen the mind."

My dad has a way of making everything fun seem like a life lesson. But I didn't care. I was getting park time with Cheerio. I couldn't wait to see what he'd think of all that grass.

We walked down 78th Street all the way to Riverside Park.

The minute Cheerio saw the grass, he took off running. I was holding the leash, and he practically pulled me off my feet.

There were so many new things for him to explore. He couldn't decide what to do first. He ran to the rocks and sniffed all around them. He ran to the tree and sniffed some more. When he found a fire hydrant, I thought his nose was going to fall off from over-sniffing.

We headed toward the basketball courts.

"Oh, look who's there shooting some hoops," my dad said. "Isn't that boy in your class? He's with his father,

who just bought the bowling
alley on Eighty-Sixth street."

When I looked over to the
basketball court, my heart sank
down to my knees. There was
Nick McKelty, shooting baskets
with his dad. Nick was the last
person I wanted to see right
now.

"Let's go say hello," my dad suggested.

"Let's not and say we did."

"Well, I'm going to say hello," my dad said. "A man with a new bowling alley is going to need some help with his computers. And, might I remind you, that is what I do for a living."

Before I could stop him, my dad had marched up to Mr. McKelty and introduced himself. Right away, they started talking about business. I don't know why grown-ups always do that. That left me and Nick McKelty staring at each other with nothing to say.

"Your dog looks like a hot dog," McKelty sneered.

Cheerio just wagged his tail happily. I guess some puppies don't know a jerk when they see one.

"I bet he feels like one, too," McKelty added.

Then he bent down to touch Cheerio. But instead of petting him, he unhooked his leash from his collar! Cheerio took off running.

"Come back, Cheerio!" I yelled as he chased a fat gray squirrel around the park.

But Cheerio wasn't interested in listening. All he was thinking about was catching that squirrel.

"Hank!" my father called out. "Get your dog!"

I went after him, but I couldn't catch him. No matter which direction I went, Cheerio ran the opposite way. To him, it was a game.

McKelty just stood there laughing his head off.

"You are such a loser, Zippertooth," he said under his breath as I ran by him for the fifth time.

My dad joined in the chase. He ran after Cheerio, but he didn't have any more success than I did. A mom pushing a stroller stepped out of the way so he could run by her. Two little kids on the swings just pointed and laughed.

Cheerio never got tired. Finally, he stopped right next to the fountain to catch his breath. Panting hard, he looked up at the statue in the middle of it. It's a statue of a man on a horse. I think Cheerio thought he could play with the horse, because he jumped right into the fountain.

"Now I've got you cornered!"

my dad yelled. And with that,
he jumped into the fountain, too,
shoes and all. A tourist with
a camera stopped taking pictures
of his wife and started shooting
pictures of my dad.

"These New Yorkers know how
to have fun," I heard him say.

Cheerio just splashed around in the shallow water. He was having the best time. My dad was not. With every step, he splashed himself more and more, until he was dripping wet. Even the mechanical pencils in his shirt pocket got soaked.

"This is it, buddy!" he roared at Cheerio. "Your playtime is over!"

He plunged into the water.
When he came up for air, he was
holding two things. Cheerio was
in one hand, and a large goldfish
was in the other.

"Hey, Dad, you're quite a
fisherman," I called out.

My father did not crack a
smile. His face was purple with

anger. He climbed out of the fountain and put Cheerio back on his leash.

"Come on, Hank," he growled. "I have to get out of these wet clothes."

"Dad, just let me explain what happened," I said.

"Not now, Hank. You've gotten into enough trouble for one day."

We walked home in total silence. Even Cheerio knew not to make a peep. When we reached Broadway and 78th Street, I tried to start a conversation.

"You're shivering, Dad," I said. "Do you want to borrow my jacket?

"It's a little small, but you could wear it as a scarf," I continued.

Again, no answer.

In fact, he didn't speak until we got to the elevator in our building. Then he turned to me and said the sentence I was hoping he wouldn't say.

"This 'adventure' proves that you are not ready to take care of a dog," he said. "I specifically told you that you were to keep Cheerio on the leash at all times. And yet, you couldn't follow even that simple rule."

"But it wasn't my fault, Dad."

"Not another word, Hank. This dog is going back to the animal shelter."

"No, Dad! Please! No!" I was trying as hard as I could not to cry.

"Hank, that is my decision," he said. "End of story."

CHAPTER 11

When we got home, the first thing my dad did was put Cheerio in his crate. Then he took a shower to wash off the fountain water. After he put on some dry clothes, he came into the living room.

"Dad," I said. I had been waiting for him. "You've got to give Cheerio another chance. Please."

He didn't answer, just walked

into the dining room. I followed right behind him.

"I've only known him for one day, Dad, and he's already my best friend," I pleaded.

"Then you should have taken better care of him," my dad said. "Letting him off the leash was very dangerous for him."

"But, Dad . . ."

He picked up his phone and turned his back to me.

"You're not calling the animal shelter, are you, Dad?" I asked nervously.

"Not yet," he answered.

"Good," I said. "Then are you calling for a pizza?"

"Hank, I'm calling to invite

Rick McKelty over," he said.
"Your dog interrupted a very
important business conversation
that we have to finish. I'll
call the animal shelter in the
morning."

I listened as he arranged
for Mr. McKelty to come
over. I hoped that after their
conversation, I'd have another
chance to change my dad's
mind.

I went into my room and threw
myself onto my bed. When I
thought about losing Cheerio,
I couldn't hold in my tears
any longer. I cried so much
that my pillow got soaking wet.

I don't know how long I lay

there crying. Finally, I got up
and blew my nose about twenty
times. Then I called Frankie
to talk over the situation, but
his mom said he was out at his
karate lesson. I called Ashley.
When I got a recording saying,
"The Wongs aren't available
to take your call," I hung up
without even leaving a message.
Then I tried calling Papa Pete.

He wasn't home, either. Where was everyone when I needed them the most?

I heard the intercom buzzer ringing in the living room.

"Hank!" my father called. "That must be Rick McKelty. Please buzz him in. Tell him I'm just printing out a few papers for us to go over."

The buzzer rang again.

"Hank!" my father called. "Do it now!"

I went into the living room and spoke into the intercom.

"Come on up," I said, my nose sounding all stuffy. "Tenth floor."

When Rick McKelty stepped

out of the elevator a few
minutes later, he was not
alone. By his side was his
troublemaker son.

 "My dad's
here to hire
your dad," Nick
the Tick said, a
smirk plastered
across his large
face. Then he
walked right past me and into
our living room.

"Where's your stupid dog?"
he asked me.

"He's locked in his crate.
And then he's going back to the
shelter, thanks to you."

Our dads had already sat down at the dining-room table to talk business.

"Your house is boring," McKelty said. "Don't you have anything fun to do here?"

Just then, Emily came out of her room, wearing Katherine around her neck like a scarf again. McKelty's eyes grew wide at the sight.

"Hey, why don't you introduce me to your lizard friend?" he said to Emily.

"She's not a lizard," Emily told him. "She's a very sensitive iguana. So please keep your voice down."

"Excuse me for breathing," Nick said.

The three of us just stood there in silence. I could hear Cheerio whimpering behind the kitchen door.

"Your dog is crying like a baby," McKelty said. "What's his problem?"

"Cheerio is being punished," Emily said. "He wouldn't stay on his leash in the park."

"That's because I unhooked it." McKelty snickered.

"Why would you do that?" Emily asked.

"Seemed like it would be fun," the big creep answered.

"I wanted to see how much trouble your brother's short-legged runt could cause."

"This is what I've been trying to explain to Dad," I told Emily. "What happened in the park wasn't my fault. And it sure wasn't Cheerio's."

Emily whirled around so fast that her braids whipped me in the face. Without a word, she stormed into the dining room. Poor Katherine nearly fell off her shoulders. Her little claws had to work overtime just to hang on.

"Dad!" Emily said, putting herself right in front of his face.

"Not now, Emily," Dad said.
"I am having a business meeting."

"But, Dad, you have to hear
this. It can't wait."

My dad turned to Rick
McKelty. "I'm sorry for the
interruption," he said. Then,
turning to Emily, he asked,
"Now, *what* is so important?"

"You know Katherine and I

are not fans of Cheerio," she said. "But fair is fair."

"Emily, we can discuss the dog after the McKeltys leave," he said in a low voice.

"Mr. McKelty should hear this, too," she told him. "It wasn't Hank who let Cheerio off the leash. It was Nick. He did it just to be mean. And he admitted it right there in the living room. Didn't he, Katherine?"

Katherine shot out her tongue and hissed.

"You see?" Emily said. "Katherine never lies."

I felt like I needed to wash out my ears. I couldn't believe what I was hearing. Emily, the one who never wanted Cheerio in the first place, was coming to his rescue. Even Katherine was defending him. I never realized what a great reptile she was.

"Nick," Mr. McKelty said, "is this true?"

"What's the big deal, Dad?" McKelty answered. "I thought the dog needed some exercise."

"Nick, that's not a decision for you to make." His dad sounded angry. "That pet does not belong to you."

Rick McKelty stood up and collected his papers from the table.

"Stan," he said, "we'll continue our business at another

time. Right now, I'm taking Nick home. He and I are going to have a serious conversation."

One thing I know for sure. When your mom or dad says they're going to have a serious conversation with you, nothing good happens.

I flashed Nick my best Zipzer smile.

"Enjoy your chat," I whispered.

When they were gone, I turned to my dad.

"Hank, I owe you an apology," he said.

I shook my head to make sure I wasn't wearing someone else's ears. But they were mine, all right.

"You tried to tell me the truth about what happened in the park," he went on. "And I didn't listen. I thought I knew what had happened, but I was wrong. I shouldn't have blamed you until I had the facts. I'm sorry, Hank."

I ran to my dad and threw my arms around his neck.

"I am so happy right now, I could scream," I said. And then I did.

"So does this mean we can keep Cheerio?" I asked him.

"This means you have to continue to step up to the plate," he answered.

What was he talking about?

I don't even play baseball.

"Cheerio can stay," he explained, "but only if I continue to see improvement in your grades. That was our agreement. Remember, I said all your grades had to improve, not just a few. That was the deal, and I expect you to keep it."

To me, that sounded like a yes.

CHAPTER 12

I asked my mom to make sure she was home at exactly six thirty. I invited Papa Pete, Frankie, and Ashley over, too. They all arrived on time.

I asked everyone to sit on the living-room floor in a big circle. I didn't even object when Emily brought Katherine. I wanted all my family and friends there.

After the whole group was gathered, I went into my room

to get Cheerio. I picked him up and put him on my pillow. Then I carried him into the living room and placed the pillow in the center of the circle.

"I have gathered everyone together here to welcome Cheerio into our family," I announced. Then I picked up the piece of paper I had decorated while I was waiting for everyone to come over. It was Cheerio's official birth certificate. I cleared my throat and read aloud.

"This paper says that Cheerio finally has a last name," I read. "From this day forth, he shall be known as Cheerio S. Zipzer."

"What's the *S* for?" Emily asked.

"Superdog," I answered.

"Cool name!" Frankie nodded.

"Now all he needs is a Superdog cape," Papa Pete said.

"With rhinestones," Ashley added.

My mom laughed, and everyone else joined in.
I think I saw my dad almost smile.

We celebrated with milk and cookies. While I was finishing my favorite black-and-white cookie, my dad picked up Cheerio's birth certificate.

Cherio
'S'
zipzer

Hank

"Hank," he pointed out, "you've spelled *Cheerio* wrong. There are two *E*s in his name. You'll have to rewrite this."

He handed the paper back to me.

"Sorry, Cheerio," I said. "I'm not the best speller in the world."

He didn't care. He snatched the paper out of my hand and took a big bite out of it. Then with everyone watching, he did his crazy spin. I'm pretty sure he

was telling us all how happy
he was to be a Zipzer.

"That dog is crazy," Emily
said.

"Crazy happy," I answered.
"Just like me."

CHAPTER 13

THE THREE CUTEST THINGS MY DOG, CHEERIO, DOES

By HANK ZIPZER

1. Absolutely everything.

   There is no 2 and 3.